Slowly Downward

Stanley Donwood was born in Essex, England,
and lived there until he was able to leave.
His employment history is patchy and insubstantial,
although he has worked briefly and unsuccessfully as a
dishwasher at an extremely unpleasant restaurant, at the Post
Office, and at various archæological digs; and then in the
black economy as a farm labourer, an envelope-stuffer and a
forestry worker. But mostly as a farm labourer.
Following several years as a graffitti-painting 'jobseeker',
he began to travel England as an itinerant fire-breather, but
the poor financial returns coupled with the rumour that
swallowing paraffin can cause pleurisy forced him to abandon
the trade. It was at about this time that he began to make
record covers for the band Radiohead, and from then on it
was a life of champagne, first-class flights, award ceremonies,
limousines, exclusive hotels and the inevitable ennui.
The author's other publications include *Catacombs of
Terror!, Tachistoscope,* and *Walking from Great Bedwyn to
Avebury,* a publication which ran to only 10 copies. He is
currently working on two new books, to be entitled
respectively *Household Worms* and *Folly.*
Stanley currently divides his time between the bleak
marshes of the East, and the equally bleak moors of the West.

Nobody likes nothing.
I certainly wish with all my heart
that it did not exist. But wishing is not enough.
We live in the real world, where nothing does exist.
We cannot just 'disinvent' it.

Nothing is not comprehensible: neither you nor I
have any hope of understanding just what it is
and what it does.

It is hard to know if nothing is actually nothing,
and thus difficult to know if a policy
of doing nothing is successful.

Nothing, however effective it may have proved up
to the present, can hardly continue to do so indefinitely.
If I had to choose between the continued possibility
of nothing happening and of doing nothing,
I would unquestionably choose the latter.

Or the former.

A Note on the Type.

This book is set in Caslon, *'the oldest living typeface'*. This type has remained in almost exactly the same form as when it was hand-cut by William Caslon *(b. 1692 or 1693)* in Ironmonger Row, London in 1722. Prior to this date, most of the type used in England was brought in from Holland, as for many years printing had been prohibited outside London and the university centres of Cambridge and Oxford, and the printing industry was in the doldrums.

Caslon's typefaces were based on the Dutch old style types, but his work marked a turning point in English type-founding. His typefaces had *"a quality of interest, a variety of design, and a delicacy of modelling which few Dutch types posessed... To say precisely how Caslon arrived at his effects is not simple; but he did so because he was an artist".**

Caslon's new English style was widely admired, and in America was used for both the *Declaration Of Independence* in 1776 and later the *United States Constitution*.

William Caslon died in 1766, but his foundry remained in the family for another century. The last of the Caslons to be active in the firm died in 1874, but the Caslon typeface remains, used in books, magazines and advertising, to the present date.

Among typographers there is an *'almost superstitious regard'* for this typeface.

* Daniel Berkeley Updike, *Printing Types, Their History, Forms, And Use* (Harvard University Press, 1937).

Further reading:
Alexander Lawson, *Anatomy Of A Typeface* (Hamilton, 1990);
Mac McGrew, *American Metal Typeafces Of The Twentieth Century* (Oak Knoll Books, 1993); Simon Loxley, *Type: The Secret History Of Letters* (I.B. Taurus, 2004)

STANLEY DONWOOD

Slowly Downward

Small Thoughts

A Bit Worried Today

Partly Mechanical Hardly Human

Two Substances

Illustrated by
Adam Rickwood

NoSuch
Library Editions

This collection first published by *Hedonist Books*, May 1st, 2001.

Trouble With Neighbours first appeared in *The Hedonist* (June 1996).

On Sundays Ringroad Supermarket first appeared in
NoData Personal Surveillance Document (fStop, 1997).

*Seaside Town of Vampires, New Job, Chip Shop, Laboratory, Aztec
Procession, Game, Fingers, Futile Gesture, Dizzy Spell* and *Burning Pub*
first appeared in *A Tin of Small Thoughts* (1998).

Chip Shop and *New Job* also appeared in
Airbag / How Am I Driving, released by *Radiohead* (1998).

Some of these stories have also appeared in
IDEA magazine (Tokyo) and in *TANK* magazine (London).

Illustrations by Adam Rickwood.

Text designed and set by Ambrose Blimfield.
Cover and flyleaf photography by Danielle Chanel.

ISBN 0-9544177-3-9

Slowly Downward

Second edition published 2001.
Third edition published 2004.

This edition published in England in 2005
by Naked Guides Limited,
The Studio, The Little Theatre Cinema, Bath, Somerset.
www.nakedguides.co.uk

Printed by Short Run Press, Exeter, Devon.

www.slowlydownward.com

Probably these stories should be printed on small pieces of paper and left blu-tacked inside phone booths with all the other prostitutes' cards.

"Slender story, new in town,
willing to service bored visitors."

For M + I + K

Contents

A Bit Worried Today

Partly Mechanical, Hardly Human

Two Substances

Foreword by Ric Jerrom, Esq.

I find myself in a dank underground chamber whose stone walls ooze a ghastly muculent slime. A scant fathom of wrecked and wretched gothic masonry separates us from the charnel pit where a crush of contorted cadavers sleeps unquietly, luckless victims of experimental surgery during the Age of Enlightenment. "Us?"

In the pallid glimmer of a guttering candle, 33 pairs of mournful eyes squinny balefully at me, as a hollow voice intones sonorously. *My* voice, I realise, hopelessly, reading aloud once more the dark tormented musings of Stanley Donwood, that Brautigan of the bestial. His words, my voice: hapless, helpless. Through the foetid miasm comes the awful sound of sardonic sniggers as some doomed soul catches a hint of ghoulish "humour" amidst Donwood's tenebrous text.

Welcome to the Lugubrium.

9 June 2005

Small Thoughts

New Job

After a tortured night I awake full of determination.

I review my position, and consider with circumspect gravity my inner strength. My new job demands much, and I eat my breakfast whilst wearing a serious and adult expression. I suck the hot coffee with a professionally pained mouth, and flip the pages of my broadsheet nonchalantly.

I swoop back up the stairs in my towelling dressing-gown, and fling open my wardrobe in a manner which I assume to be casual and easy. My suit hangs in front of me, full of nothing. It is up to me to fill it with myself.

I pull on the trousers, and carefully fold my penis behind the zip, fastening the button with what I hope is a manly grin. I tuck my shirt into the trousers, and spend some time with my understated tie.

My jacket feels slightly small under my arms, but it is nothing anyone would notice.

I wonder what my new workmates will be like, and fantasise briefly about the relationships I may possibly enjoy with other members of the organisation.

I glance once again at my digital watch, and decide that I am ready. I pull on my coat, check that I have my keys, and walk out of the front door, slamming it firmly behind me.

I stand outside, looking blankly ahead, realising I don't have a new job at all.

Bond James Bond

The world is at terrible risk from hideous and malevolent alien monsters and it is up to me to do something about it.

Luckily I stumble across an alien podule which can take me up to the huge war satellite that is circling Earth. It is a squeeze, but I get into the podule and quickly comprehend the alien dashboard and launch into space.

Within minutes I dock with the war satellite and effect my egress. The satellite is a maze of chrome corridors, and I creep along them in my silent, rubber-soled shoes.

I take my Beretta from inside my dinner-jacket as I hear a faint cough in the distance. I pass along more corridors and through several chrome rooms the size of cathedrals until I near my quarry.

I peer around a doorway and am surprised to see a famous professor from Earth. Swiftly I attack him. When I kick him in the stomach, he collapses like a sack of heavy air.

I pull him to his feet and interrogate him. It seems that he has been creating alien monsters with an evil alien academic who wants to take over the planet Earth. At first he assumed the alien was well-intentioned, but the monsters they made were increasingly violent and deranged.

He introduces me to his first monster, who is very courteous, but I am told that all the subsequent monsters would tear my head off at the slightest provocation. I decide to let the professor go for the time being, and hefting my Beretta, I go in search of my nemesis.

Nearly Got

One night I am alone in my house, compiling lists of friends from the past. It grows dark, and I begin to wish for company. The list sits before me on the table, reproaching me with intimations of missed opportunities and regretful abandonments.

There is a scratching at the window, and absently I open it, assuming that one of my cats is feeling lonely too. To my dismay, a small devil-creature, salivating with anticipation, leaps squatly into the room. I recognise it immediately as being of the type to possess the soul without hesitation.

Backing away from its gleaming eyes, I consider my options. With a flash of intelligence, I announce to the devil-creature that it is yesterday, and today I am dead. The creature looks quizzically at me. I insist that it has made an error - it is yesterday, and later this evening I kill myself with a large, sharp kitchen knife. I am dead. My soul has gone. The devil-creature is too late.

It looks puzzled, but I explain, with placatory hand movements, that this is really a simple matter. As I am already dead, there is no point in attempting to take my soul. Come back in a week, I tell the devil-creature. The landlord will have re-let the house, and there will be fresh prey.

Huffing and puffing, the creature waddles back to the window, and lurches off into the night.

Congratulating myself on my quick thinking, I close the window, and it is with a heavy heart that I wander into the kitchen and begin rifling through the knife drawer.

Aliens Again

I am visiting relatives of some obscure variety on their farm, which huddles in the coruscating heat of a country placed somewhere between Arizona and Nevada, but oddly reminiscent of Norfolk, England.

The news comes in that hostile Aliens from Outer Space are invading the planet. This revelation causes some alarm amongst my relatives, but not, I feel, as much as it should. Close to panic myself, I decide to escape by bicycle, and I pedal from the farm out into the bleak, sunny wheatfields.

I soon learn that the Aliens have arrived in three sorts of Space Ship. The first two kinds are enormous, although they seem to pose no immediate threat. But the third sort, which look like huge metal hot-air balloons strung with flailing steel hawsers, are another matter entirely. I realise that the first two types are dormitory craft and genetic breeding stations where cruel and foul things are carried out, and the third type is a killing machine that will throttle the life out of you for no reason whatsoever.

I cycle faster as I hear an infernal whine from the skies. Ugly shadows scud over the wheatfields, and as I watch, stringy red tentacles descend from the hovering balloon. A hapless farmhand is snatched screaming from his tractor.

I am forced to hide a number of times, and eventually my resolve to escape weakens.

After a hazardous and terrifying journey, I arrive back at the farm. Breathless, I tell my relatives that there is no hope for the human race. Again, the reaction is not quite what it should be.

Dracula

It is summer, and I am persuaded to take a continental holiday by two enthusiastic acquaintances. Being a creature of habit, I am accustomed to vacations in the seaside resorts near to my home, but the proposition is put in such a way that I find it hard to make excuses.

We depart, and travel by train to Romania, where, after a series of misadventures, we are all captured by Count Dracula, Prince of Darkness. We are taken in a foul-smelling horse-drawn carriage to his castle, which towers blasphemously above the forests, fingering the torn sky with its crumbling turrets. We are, naturally, rent with terror. It is clear that the Count intends to drink our blood, turning us into undead monsters of the night in the process.

We are imprisoned in once luxurious apartments, overlooking Dracula's estate. It is evident that the twentieth century has not treated our host well.

Ominously, he tells us in heavily-accented English that he has been forced to open up large tracts of his estate as a theme park, with log flumes, bowling alleys, rollercoasters, and burger bars, all of which are frequented by Western tourists who know nothing of the old ways.

Our sympathy is tempered by the sure knowledge

that the Count intends to suck out our souls with his pointy teeth.

We secretly devise a daring plan to flee. We encourage the Count to show us round the theme park, and, as we come to the bowling alley, hurl ourselves down the planks into the skittley darkness. We scramble through wires, pipes, and other obstructions until we find ourselves in an area devoted to crazy golf, where we mingle with the tourists. It is with some relief that we exit through the turnstiles. It is easy thence to find a hire car, and complete our courageous escape.

Back home in Eastbourne, I wonder if we did the right thing. It infuriates me that Dracula may have needed my soul more than I do.

A Man Who Thinks He Is A Pig

Accidentally, I am a guest of some sort at a shabby farm. My host is a curious elderly man with a fascination for anthropology. As soon as I arrive, he regales me with stultifying tales of his years as an explorer and ethnographer. It is all I can do to stay awake. There are two other guests at the farm, a large, big-boned man and his boyfriend, a man with an expensive haircut.

Two days pass, and I am sitting on the dilapidated veranda with the big-boned man, drinking gin. Our host shuffles over from one of the barns, and invites us to come and meet a man who thinks he is a pig. Intrigued, we put down our gins and follow to the barn. After our eyes adjust to the dim light, we find ourselves in a disgusting, reeking sty. In the gloom, we make out a man covered with mud and excrement, snuffling loudly in the steaming straw. He looks at us, grins broadly, and grunts several times. Our host tells us that the pig-man likes us.

We settle down on the filthy ground and watch as the pig-man start to fling mud about. My big-boned companion seems quite taken with the idea of becoming a pig as he hurriedly removes his shirt and grabs a handful of mud. As lumps of stinking matter fly perilously close, I decide to make a hurried exit. I effect my egress, and emerge blinking in the daylight outside. Wiping spatters of slime from my person, I return to my gin, shaking my head and wondering how on Earth I always end up surrounded by lunatics and maniacs of one sort or another.

Later that evening, drinking yet more gin and watching the setting sun, I am set upon by the man with the costly hair, who accuses me of leading his boyfriend astray. He screams to me that his once-polite partner now believes he is a pig, and then commences a vigorous and sustained physical attack.

Needless to say, I cut my 'holiday' short and return to my room in the city. There I brood on the nature of relaxation, and the fact that my recuperative powers are perhaps deformed in some horrible way.

Futile Gesture

I find myself in a responsible position within a reputable institution, and my evening arrival at home is welcomed by my beautiful wife. We share many interests, and spend pleasantly frequent hours discussing cultural matters. Our house is more than adequate for our needs, although we both ruefully agree that if we were ever to have children a relocation could be in order. But in the meantime we enjoy our life together.

One evening I am suddenly conscious of a noise from the kitchen. I ask my wife to pause the video, and pace uneasily towards the door. I walk softly in my stockinged feet. I pick up an empty wine bottle and slowly turn the handle. I feel more animal than human, more ready to deal with an intruder than I ever have before. I burst open the door, the neck of my wine bottle in my clenched fist.

There is nobody in the kitchen. I give the back yard a cursory check, but the flat feeling I have tells me that nothing will be there.

Determined to make something of my foolishness, I pointlessly grate some Edam cheese. I almost continue the grating until my fingers are bleeding, but I decide that it would be a futile gesture.

I return to the living room for the rest of the video, leaving the Edam to curl and atrophy in the kitchen.

A Quiet Afternoon

I am alone in a hot city. My favourite bar is closed for siesta, and I am aimlessly walking the dusty streets. Outside a shabby tailor's, I am accosted by a man in a dark suit. He acts in a conspiratorial manner, and invites me to follow him along the street.

After some time, we arrive at a small bar on the edge of the city. We take a seat each, and the man whispers to me that he is suffering from an unusual complaint, in that he is consistently late for everything. He explains that this is because somebody has stolen his today, forcing him to take up residence in tomorrow. As a consequence, every engagement he makes can never be honoured. He is always late, and wakes up in the morning with a terrible sense of guilt and failure. When he saw me outside the tailors, he recognised a kindred spirit, he tells me.

I tell him that he is quite mistaken: I may be renowned for my lateness, but I have been on time on occasion, and no-one has stolen my today. This visibly disappoints the man in the dark suit, and he makes his apologies and shuffles off, out of the bar. I am left feeling a little guilty, but I reassure myself that there is nothing to feel bad about.

That night, I am seized with the idea that someone has stolen my today. I find, the next day, that I have missed all my appointments by twenty-four hours.

At siesta, I see a man in a dark suit greeting an acquaintance with a firm handshake and a smile. I overhear the words, *"Glad you could make it"*.

Game

I am disturbed to discover that my colleagues have invented a new game which seems to involve attempting to kill me in every juvenile way that presents itself to them. They delight in surprising me with shoves into the paths of oncoming double-decker buses, constructing ridiculous rope-and-pulley devices with the aim of dropping heavy furniture on my head, placing tripwires at the tops of escalators, and other such inanities.

They persist for some weeks, during which I become increasingly adept at avoiding sudden death by blackly humorous means. I feel that my senses are sharpened day by day, that my sight is keener, my reflexes quicker.

Soon I can detect by the smell of linseed oil alone the presence of a cricket-bat wielding acquaintance in the bathroom. Everything is enhanced. Colours are richer, noises are louder. I awaken to the pattern of life, the weight of deeds.

Eventually my heightened awareness evolves into a vividly focused paranoia. I can only retreat; I move surreptitiously to a small seaside resort on the east coast and wait, slowly, for a death of my own choosing.

Trouble With Neighbours

The hazards of city life take their toll, and I move to a small seaside town built of wooden houses.

Unfortunately, I become involved in a dispute with my next-door neighbour. That matter escalates to the point where he feels the need to involve his hard-drinking friends.

One evening, drowning my sorrows at the tavern, I learn that my neighbour plans to burn down my house. The information distresses me considerably, and I decide to take evasive action. Returning to my house, I turn on all the taps, and with a hose I drench the walls and contents of the building. I sneak out of the flooded kitchen and hide in nearby sand-dunes.

Sure enough, later that night my neighbour and a gang of angry drunks approach my house with flaming torches. In vain, they try to set fire to the soaking wooden structure, but it is simply too wet to catch light. Hidden in the dunes, I chuckle with delight at having outwitted my neighbour.

The next day, in the grocery store, I am pinned to the wall by the shopkeeper. He tells me he is good friends with my neighbour, and accuses me of underhand tricks. I tell him I don't know what he means, but he says no-one but me would deliberately drench their own house with water simply to spoil his neighbour's fun. He tells me that killjoys like me have no place in a real community.

At home I sit on the wet sofa, pondering the nature of my existence. Later I wander the house, turning off the taps, one by one.

Dizzy Spell

Due to health problems, I find myself renting a shack-like house on the border between Mexico and Texas. The sitting-room is in the United States, whilst the kitchen is in South America. I exist on a mixed diet of Twinkies and tortillas, mulling over my emotional difficulties and awaiting a selection of telephone calls which never come. Time passes without comment, and a rusty film of disinterest forms over my thoughts.

Over a period of vaguely discernible weeks, I develop a species of vertigo which leaves me unable to look either up or down without extreme dizziness. My vision is locked on a horizontal plane. My situation deteriorates until I cannot look at the window without seeing the word *'window'* and a foggy reflection of my own countenance. Eventually I cannot enter the United States without being overcome by emotions which manifest themselves as an overwhelming compulsion to whirl around smashing everything. When I retreat to the kitchen I find mountains of crockery coated with a mixture of coagulated food and thick dust.

I huddle in the short hallway that occupies the space between the USA and Mexico, quivering with fatigue.

I cannot find my tenancy agreement. I realise that I will be stuck here, in this hallway, forever.

An Accident Involving Trellis

One hot afternoon, whilst struggling with an anthology of South American poetry, I receive a telephone call from a friend. I am invited to a garden party, to take place that evening. Relieved to be dragged away from the largely incomprehensible verse of Chile, I get changed, pour myself a large whisky, and stare for some time at the roof-tops visible from my room. The evening comes, and I stroll over to the party.

The smell of a barbecue, the chatter of voices in the summer air, and the sight of a full table of wine bottles fills me with a childlike glee, which I conceal for the sake of propriety. I spot a number of old friends and colleagues, and mingle with ease. Birds sing, audible during short lulls in conversation.

After several large glasses of wine, my bladder begins to feel a little uncomfortable, and I saunter off in search of the lavatory. After urinating, I drop a sheet of toilet paper into the bowl, the sight of tissue succumbing to water always being one of my minor pleasures in life.

I return to the party, but during my brief absence my friends have apparently been replaced by zombie doll-creatures from some long-forgotten nightmare. They look the same as ever, but exude evil.

Something is dreadfully wrong. They fail to notice me, so I scurry back into the toilet and stand, with my head resting on the cool tiles.

I come to the relentlessly adult conclusion that I must have imagined something nasty, and that all I need to do is go back out there and continue with this lovely party. Reluctantly, I return to the garden, but this time the zombies have mutated once more into slavering hell-hounds with five eyes. With a rising moan, I turn and crash through the fence, trailing broken trellis, wreathed with nasturtiums.

I awake in hospital, wondering exactly what it is that has conspired to make my life so patently unlivable.

Aztec Procession

I am sitting outside my favourite bar, drinking coffee and smoking quietly. In the distance, through the heat and softly settling dust of siesta-time, I hear a faint clattering and chanting. I turn towards the sound, straining my ears.

After several minutes have brought the noise closer, I realise that it is the music of a grand religious procession of some kind.

My suspicions are confirmed when a colourful scene bursts into the stillness of the square. In the centre of a mass of Aztecs are a royal couple, hoisted up on an elaborate double throne. The Aztecs are all expressionless, their eyes blank and dead as they chant and sing.

I glance nervously around, but I am the only person in the square. The bar appears long-closed, and my coffee is cold. As the Aztecs turn to stare vacantly at me, I feel certain that I should be elsewhere.

I unfold from my chair and bolt along a narrow alleyway between tall buildings, the washing lines flapping high above my head as the baleful roar of the Aztecs echoes from the square. I run this way and that, my heart pounding and my face streaming with sweat. I am lost, and in a blindly unreasoning panic.

On Sundays Ring Road Supermarket

I am queuing at my nearest out-of-town supermarket when an unpleasant scene begins to develop. Three shop assistants haul a muscular but dead young bullock out from behind the translucent flaps that guard the inner sanctum of the store, and lay it on the tiles in the tights, socks, and toothcare aisle. Another assistant emerges with several large knives, and the four of them stand around the carcass as if awaiting silent instructions.

As one, they flash their knives and one of them makes a large cut in the hide of the bullock. Another slices deftly at the neck area, while the third and fourth make incisions around the jaw. The two assistants nearest the head lay their now bloody knives on the clean tiles, and, with visible effort, insert their fingers into the gashes they have just made. They begin to pull at the thick, hairy skin of the bullock, tugging hard until the flesh begins to pinkly emerge. They pull and pull, and the hide slides back over the jaw. As the skin comes back, to my horror, the bullock's eyes begin to flicker.

At the moment the hide rips back over the eyes, they widen, and the bullock staggers to its feet. The assistant pull harder and harder, but the bullock charges away towards the delicatessen counter, its face flapping wildly around its flayed skull.

I am close to fainting, although I cannot, as I have been queuing at the checkout for what seems like an age. At last, my items are scanned and I pay for them, my Visa card shaking in my hand.

Love Story

I am driving a fast car along the beautiful cliffs that line the road between London and Brighton. My mind is aflame with lust.

To my left gleams the azure Mediterranean, while on my right the chalk cliffs flash in the sunlight. I am increasingly worried as the car gathers speed, as it seems that my brakes have been sabotaged.

Faster and faster, the cliffs flick past. I am forced to do some clever manoeuvering until I skilfully skid to a halt in Brighton, where my lover awaits, resplendent in a velvet-lined apartment overlooking the shingle beach.

We engage in inventive sexual games while hooligans roam the wet streets below us.

Down In The Tube Station

Far below the familiar world of the underground train system is an antiquated system constructed entirely of wood.

On a quest to find a party hosted by some loose acquaintances, I hurry through Camden Tube and take a series of very wrong turnings, then find myself alone on a tatty wooden platform. The quality of the silence that surrounds me is disturbing. I have not heard so little ever before in my life.

After what seems like an interminable wait, a uniformed official dawdles towards me along the platform. As he approaches, I notice that he is cobwebbed and extremely dusty. He says to me, in a broken whisper, that the train will be *"along presently"*.

My experience teaches me that this phrase is extremely flexible and could be interpreted in a number of ways.

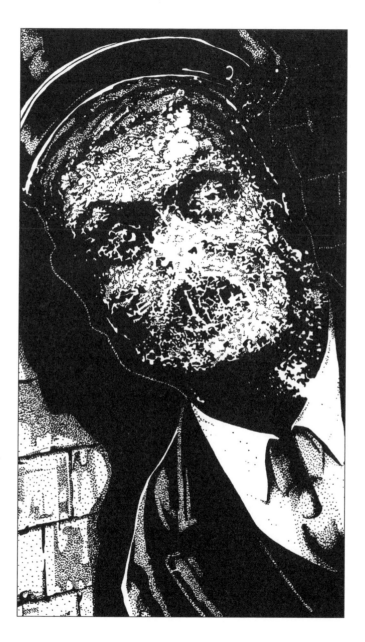

Acting With Certainty

I find myself alone in a frightening building at the dead of night. I am filled with an eerily familiar mixture of fear and rage. I reason that I could either curl up on the floor and whine pathetically or take responsibility for my inner anxieties and act with certainty.

I decide on the latter, and call out the name of my personal demon and psychic tormentor. I repeat this shout with increasing volume several times, until he appears, reeking of evil and smouldering foully.

My fury overcomes a sudden feeling of spiders crawling in my duodenum, and I launch myself at the demon, screaming an assortment of obscenities, pummelling him viciously. As I punch, he seems to diminish in size. I continue to beat him, until there is nothing left of him except his Doctor Marten boots, which I fling from the window into the night with a callous laugh.

Subsequently, I am unable to sleep at nights, as I worry greatly that there may have been something of the demon still left in the toes of the boots. I attempt to find them, but the frightening house is not on any street in my town. Weary now from sleeplessness, I wait in my room for the demon to return, and regret deeply having behaved so decisively.

Machete

I work as a personal body guard and I am employed by a gentleman who fears for his life, threatened, as he is, by dark threats of sickening violence delivered by unknown persons over the telephone.

After some preliminary investigations, it becomes clear that the telephone calls are an invention produced by the imagination of my client. Nonetheless, his fear is real and I begin to wonder if, despite appearances, there may be some truth in his fears.

My hunch proves right when, one night, my client's guttural screaming summons me to his bedroom. There, shifting from foot to foot and hyperventilating with feral excitement, is a foul creature from the underworld. The demon takes one look at me and seems to dismiss me as a minor player in this drama. He is wielding a large machete at my client, relishing the fear this engenders. My client is blubbering at me to do something.

In fact, I had suspected that demons may have been at the bottom of this job, and have taken the precaution of acquiring a phony machete of flimsy wooden manufacture. I tease the demon with childish taunts, and, as he rushes at me, I dextrously swap the machetes.

It is only very slightly later, when my client's head is sliced off, that I realise I have made an error. My career is finished.

A Wet Night

I am invited to a party which is being hosted by some old friends. As usual, I get to the party early and stand awkwardly outside the gates to the house. It is dark but warm, and unknown creatures speak to one another in the night.

I step hesitantly into the overgrown garden, and notice a light on in the house. Although the party may not have started, I convince myself that my hosts need help with the preparations. I am a dab hand at samosas.

Easing my way through the conifers that bar my progress, I approach the lighted house. Intending to play a minor joke, I peer in through the window, and I am surprised to see two Aliens from Outer Space conversing in the drawing-room. They appear to be engrossed in a clever discussion, and I withdraw quietly, not wanting to disturb them.

After loitering outside the front gate for some time, I make my way back home, now sure that the party is either not going to happen or that I have inadvertently entered another dimension.

About a week later, I come across one of my old friends in a cafe. He asks me why I wasn't at their party. I make my excuses and leave.

My brother calls me at home, and we discuss our

respective social lives. My brother complains of a boredom with life, while I counterpoint with a distrust of parties in general and clever Aliens in particular. Eventually, we agree to finish the conversation, but as I put the phone on the hook I am seized with terror.

Quivering, I run a bath, aware that both my reactions and my emotions are ill-placed.

Rubbish Time Machine

Having at last completed work on my time machine, I am disappointed to find that it does not work beyond the parameters of my own life. I can travel back to my childhood years, observe myself behaving insufferably as a teenager, see myself as a tottering octogenarian; in effect I can visit any period of my relatively mundane life, but cannot travel to the past that I missed or the future I will never see. To compound this problem, I cannot actually touch, taste or smell anything during my already uninteresting travels.

No-one in the past or future can see me. I attempt to speak with myself, warn myself about imminent dangers, shout *don't marry her*, and so on, but all that escapes the confines of my mouth are little puffs of carbon dioxide. The whole time travel thing seems horribly reminiscent of my experience at parties.

Back in my laboratory, I extricate myself from the spidery apparatus of the time machine, and stare wearily from the bleary windows.

Burning Pub

Whilst drinking coffee in my usual bar I am joined by a group of friends. A couple of hours pass in a pleasant manner, and as evening darkens the sky I am persuaded to join them for a bibulous meander.

As the sun creases into a bank of simmering cumulus, consensus decrees that we visit a bar close to the meat-packing district. A relatively brief walk, and our destination is within sight. Pigeons scutter overhead, and I am reminded of my jacket which I must collect from the dry-cleaners. The blackened city curves over our passage, and we halt for a group consultation of the A to Z.

I notice a flash of light in the corner of my vision, and turn swiftly. Across the road, within the plate-glass windows of a large and busy pub, sudden flames billow and swoop towards the ceiling. I stare, clamped to the pavement with disbelief. A surge of light blasts from the pub windows, which are now completely filled with incandescence. I stand open-mouthed, unable to communicate the horror that is coursing through me, merely ullulating monosyllabically. As suddenly as they flared, the flames disappear.

Within the pub, the customers continue their

evening. With gasping breaths, I attempt to explain what I have just seen to my friends.

It is a nuclear holocaust theme pub, they explain. Nothing is real. I am unable to deal with this, and make my way home through the echoing streets with tearful eyes.

Machine

For some reason I am in a vast, disused seedling nursery where grim and dilapidated glasshouses sprout from the barren and debris-strewn ground. Each is home to a different contraption whose function is wholly unclear.

I am escorted by silent, hooded people to one of the glasshouses. In it squats a machine approximately thirty feet long, which, it is explained to me, is used to make paintings of body parts.

Into one end of the machine the hooded people insert hands which have been severed from corpses. A series of clunks and hisses are emitted by the machinery, then a collection of small paintings of hands are deposited from the other end. The paintings are quite beautiful, and are reminiscent of the Fauvist tradition. The dusty walls of the glasshouse are haphazardly hung with many of these works.

After watching the operation of the machine with polite interest for some time, it occurs to me that this may not have been its intended function. With sudden enthusiasm, I explain to my hosts that during the early years of photographic invention, the process was not thought to be simply a matter of developing an image and fixing it. In the later years of the Nineteenth Century, developed photographs were merely a stage in the entire process of producing paintings by mechanical means, using machines of the type now seen before us.

After I give this explanation, the hooded people turn to me with perhaps even greater silence than they have employed so far. I am firmly escorted from the premises. I am handed a small card which tells me that my interpretation is not welcome, and that I am forbidden from ever visiting again.

I feel a hopeless sense of failure, and once home, set about destroying all my photographic impedimenta.

Big Bird

Whilst on a walking holiday in remote regions, I chance upon a secluded valley, away from the popular walking routes. Some distance along the valley I come across a scene so breathtakingly beautiful that I drop to my knees in wonder. There is something about the serried ranks of deciduous and coniferous trees standing tall on the opposite bank of the river that sets my heart ablaze. The colours of the foliage are poetic, whilst the arrangement of species seems divinely inspired. Clouds swoop and whirl above the topmost branches, and the river sparkles through an uncertain reflection below.

Suddenly, the sky darkens, and along the river advances a flotilla of huge birds with menacing eyes. The size of the birds staggers me; one is as tall as a bus, and the others not much smaller. Their plumage is a shimmering blue, but their eyes are full of hate and looming disaster. With a horrible sinking feeling, I realise that the birds have noticed me. One of them clambers up the nearside bank, and waddles towards me.

I take to my heels, and scramble along the path. Gaining speed, I run at full tilt. Then I see people in front of me, running towards me. First one passes, then another, then another. They are wide-eyed with terror, and keep taking quick, fearful looks behind them. There must, I realise, be something unutterably horrible in front of me, but my fear of the big birds compels me to carry on.

More people run past me, all with the same frightened expression. They are running towards the birds, away from something unknown. I am running from the birds, towards something unknown.

Not for the first time in my life, I curse my bad luck.

Laboratory

I obtain a poorly-paid job in a dusty laboratory. The afternoon sunlight falls into the room through yellowing Venetian blinds, and I pass the time making tea and answering oblique questions desultorily during collapsed conversations.

As time passes in its tedious way I slowly become aware that the experiments taking place in the laboratory are at best sinister; and at worst, evil. At least eighty per cent of the hypotheses are obviously invalid and intended to support revolting surmises.

I increasingly spend most of my time in the kitchen, staring at the limescale that bedecks the overflow of the sink. I fancy that I can see emergent civilisations in the crust that grows daily around the tap bases.

The weeks fall through my fingers. Eventually the experiments become too much for me to tolerate. Mice are being sacrificed to a nameless dark presence that hovers over the building, manifesting in the dust, colouring the minds of the scientists with whom I am forced to spend my futile daylight. Somehow the laboratory is filling my dreams with fear.

I soon recognise that it is the mouldering soul of the building itself that is engineering this mounting horror. Quietly, during my tea-making duties, I plan my escape. I realise that if I mention my discontent to my co-workers all exits will be closed to me.

At last, with a daring flourish of courage, I attempt to effect my egress. It is with a dreadful terror that I realise the door is locked. I turn, and see the hollow eyes of the scientists upon me. There can be no escape.

Seaside Town Of Vampires

My holiday takes me to a resort for which I have distant but fond memories of innocent pleasures and fine bars. I wander the littered streets until I find my favourite cantina, now flyblown and murky. The proprietor fails to recognise me, and I order a coffee.

Sitting outside in the wan sunlight I am depressed by the changes that have taken place in this once beautiful seaside town. Many shops are boarded up, the youth seem preoccupied with the dusty ground, and the cinema has been transformed into a seemingly unpopular bingo hall. Worst of all are the diminutive vampires who bowl along the promenade biting the legs of passers-by. The only way to deal with these pointy-toothed parasites is to kick them viciously off the quay. I entertain myself morosely in this way for about half an hour, sustaining only slight scratches from the fangs of these riviera nosferatu.

Things are not what they used to be around here. The thought reminds me uncomfortably of my ageing body, and my own repressed desire to live vicariously the lives of others.

I realise that although I can understand the sad plight of the vampires, I cannot resist the urge to kick them, flailing, into the grey ocean.

I return to my room, and sit at the window. If there were an observer, I imagine that they might see the cloud-scattered evening sky, reflected in my dark pupils.

Fingers

It is only after I have been at my new flat for some months that I begin to receive mail other than bills and offers to enter prize draws. One of my first personal envelopes contains a scrawled message from an old acquaintance with whom I was friendly many years ago. I am distressed to read that my friend is deeply unhappy, and I am disturbed further to read that if he receives no reply to the letter I hold in my hands he will feel compelled to chop off one of his fingers with a kitchen knife.

Days pass, full of inconsequential incidents, until a small parcel arrives. The postmark indicates that it is from my friend. With trepidation I open it. Underneath the brown wrapping paper is a little box which bears the return address of my friend. There is also a stamp on the box, but other than this the package proves to be empty. I open up the box, but the space within is likewise vacant. A sense of relief floods briefly through me, and my days once more assume a comfortable aspect.

One week later, another identical parcel arrives. It too is empty, and I insist to myself that I will write to my friend. Time drifts past, and eventually I have ten empty parcels. It is on a Friday that I realise what I have to do.

With what I feel is admirable forethought I use my left hand to chop three fingers from my right. With the remaining two, I hack off all the fingers of my left hand. In considerable pain I place the fingers in eight of the parcels. There is a lot of blood, and this makes the use of Sellotape difficult.

With eight parcels wrapped, I hold the knife in my right thumb and forefinger. I look at the last two boxes. As always, it is my inability to complete any task that drives me to tears.

Statue

I am commissioned by a wealthy opera singer to carve a marble sculpture of her torso.

Without shame, she disrobes, and I make preparatory drawings, noting the lines of her voluptuous curves and the weight of her voluminous tresses.

An enormous block of marble is duly delivered to the velvety chamber where I am to carry out my trade. Confidently I take up my mallet and chisel, and begin to rough out the statue.

Days pass, then weeks, and after a period of over two months I announce to my patron that the work is complete. She stares for some time at the fruit of my endeavours. Something is not right. I sense that she is displeased in some way. I shoo her from the chamber, order another block of marble, and begin again.

I am enshrouded in dust, I work through the night, until my fingers are raw and my breath comes in harsh rasps. Again, my employer is unaccountably dissatisfied.

I continue to order marble, and continue to carve statue after statue, while the years pass.

When, eventually, I create a marble likeness of the opera singer on her deathbed with my own wizened and arthritic fingers, she at last nods, smiles, and abandons herself to the relentless pull of eternal sleep.

I place my chisels carefully on the floor, and lie next to her, placing my dusty hand in her cooling fingers.

Shopping In The Early Morning

The sun has not yet risen as I wander the convoluted streets of a city I am sure I have visited before, perhaps when I was very young. Everything is dusty, as if dew never falls here. The fact that not a soul is about adds to the unreality of the place, along with my faltering observation that there is no architecture here that dates from after about 1600.

The overhanging gables hide the bleached sky, and my hunger drives me on. I am seeking a newsagent, as for some time my erratic sleeping habits have made me reliant on these early-opening Meccas of providence. There is something definitely unwholesome about the ranges of snacks, the serried chocolate bars, the newspapers and the minority-interest pornographic magazines, but the newsagent has always seemed to me a haven from the cold, empty-stomached early hours.

The city slumbers on, and my feet cross cobbled squares, take me along twisting alleys, and into the quiet lung of the urb. There is no sign of any kind of shop at all, let alone the reassuring fluorescent experience of an Eight-Till-Late or the like. The only commercial enterprise I pass is a shoemaker's shop, festooned with dusty boots and leather offcuts.

Occasionally I glimpse the countryside, trapped between two desperately overleaning Tudor eaves.

Eventually I find what I am looking for, but, disappointingly, the stock consists of a range of Cook-In Sauces and three cans of sardines. I leave the shop with a can of sardines and return to the maze of streets, now almost certain that something is amiss.

Not Proud Of Everything

There are a lot of good things about being a vampire, but morally it's fairly indefensible. I like to think that I'm quite a reasonable sort of person. Like most people, I've done plenty of things that I'm not too proud of, and a few that I really regret. You might find it tricky to believe, but there are a fair number of people around who are attracted to vampires and vampirism as a sort of lifestyle thing, and a larger number who just don't mind dying.

Mostly, I put adverts in the personal columns, and when we meet I go to considerable lengths to explain the options and what they entail. If they're not completely into the idea, we part company there and then. Well, usually, anyway. As I say, I'm not proud of everything I've done. Sometimes things just get out of hand.

Haunted

While I am searching for an old diary in the attic, I find a large cardboard box full of ring-binders, which, in turn, are full of notes I once made concerning the construction of an emotional puncture kit. The find seems providential: my love-life is in tatters. Constructed almost entirely of half-truths, fabricated intuitions and vaguely remembered urges, my private life is transparently in desperate want of repair. If ever I needed the emotional puncture kit, it is at this emotional juncture.

Unfortunately, I need to locate several parts to build the puncture kit, and despite many pleading telephone calls to various ironmongers, greengrocers, bookmakers, stationery shops and butchers, I am unable to assemble the kit.

I look out of the window, and notice that tumbleweed is blowing past the house. The sight adds to my increasing depression, and I hasten to the town to actively seek the parts I need.

A pawnbroker's catches my eye, and I step inside the musty shop. I explain my predicament to the papery man behind the grille, and he shows me a box which houses some small rodents. The pawnbroker tells me that the rodents may not replace my love life, but they will love me if I love them. And if I fail to love them, they will punish me with their sharp pointy teeth.

Not quite knowing why, I buy the rodents and hurry home. Once there, I tell them sweet things, and get them a saucer of milk.

Later, my husband returns. It seems that he has successfully sold my old diary to a major publisher.

I am oddly unmoved, but then, I have my rodents.

Happy Story

I am unfortunately diagnosed as having a terminal disease, and that my demise is imminent. This information upsets me greatly, and my age is nowhere near sufficient to have prepared me for such news.

With many tears I sell my possessions and invest my capital in a parachute jump for myself.

Upon leaving the aeroplane, I am faced with my final decision. I opt not to pull the ripcord, and continue my descent with increasing rapidity and a slightly worried smile. I ponder on my life, such as it has been, and conclude that although the parts were varied and often tinged with sadness, the whole has a dimly beautiful shape.

Chip Shop

Despite my reservations, I am wandering the streets of the town in the company of several people with whom I have little in common. The evening has been dominated by seemingly random sallies into pubs populated almost exclusively by large men in vests, with whom I have absolutely nothing in common.

Every glance upwards reveals a sky that has been soaked the colour of undistinguished lager. Every time I attempt to join in the obvious jollity of the occasion I am drowned out by the inadvertent yelping of my compatriots, and I resort to adopting a vacuous yet friendly expression whenever any enquiry is directed in my direction.

We stand in a huddle of indecision outside a brightly-lit doorway, and earnest debate falls around my ears as I watch, with unbelieving nausea, a chef in the chip shop opposite shoo a flaming, but living, pigeon from the window of his establishment. The flying, sputtering lump of flame erupts from the window with an erratic path that is subsumed from my attention by an enquiry from my colleagues regarding money. I answer with rapidity, only to turn my gaze back to find the burning bird has disappeared from my view.

After an eternity of boredom we emerge from the club. The pigeon is lying in the gutter, curiously expanded, horribly burnt, utterly dead.

Zombie Public Limited Company

For reasons too dull or humiliating to go into, I ended up blah blah blah. Single again, embittered or whatever. I once had a passable future but it had evaded me, or blah blah blah, with the dusty streets and the bars without clocks and the blah blah blah.

One of the days, I was just sitting watching the tumbleweed and the little tornadoes of dust on the road outside.

A removal lorry pulled up and big men began carrying large articles of furniture shrouded in blankets up the steps to the empty house opposite my block.

The people or the blah blah blah, but it wasn't for about a week until I realised that they were watching me. I can't continue with this.

Give it to me straight.

I am living quietly, zombie public limited company move in over the road, the workers look at us with hungry eyes, we lock the doors but to no avail, they get in, they eat our brains, we are reborn as zombies, slaves to the company, but it turns out not so bad, being a zombie is ok, but really we want to be free or something.

I like your pitch. It's an interesting metaphor.

We'll put a package together. Create a buzz. We could be talking telephone numbers.

   [HEADS EXPLODE. BLOOD SPLATTERS EVERYWHERE. CUT TO: MTV]

Airborne

One rainy day whilst out shopping for groceries, I am surrounded by a growing crowd who are under the impression that I can fly.

It seems that a dreadful mistake has been made: the local paper has printed an article about a gentleman who really does have this enviable talent, but they have put my photograph above the article. I am unsure about how the newspaper came to have a picture of me, but that is the least of my worries, faced, as I am, with this heckling crowd of strangers. I protest, but the crowd will give no quarter until I show them my incredible powers.

At last, I give in to them, and stand, flapping my arms and jumping as high as I can into the damp air. This goes on for some time, and I become increasingly frightened that the now disenchanted crowd will attack me, believing me to be a self-promoting charlatan. But in the end they straggle off, muttering. Thanking my lucky stars, I rush home, too upset to continue my shopping.

That evening, alone, I once again try to fly. It proves to be a futile exercise, but addictive.

Night after night I stand on my roof, flapping my arms and making small jumps on the tiles. Try as I might, I never manage to get airborne.

Space

During the war I visit some relations in the country. The privations of living for years in a battle zone have hit them hard, and although the war is nearly over they remain locked into the habits of the frightened.

After a frugal meal of potato soup, I am invited to look round the smallholding that surrounds their scarred house. Oddly, in the paddock are smaller fenced areas. Puzzled, I ask why they are there. The reason is simple: each small fenced area represents an animal that has long been eaten. The fences are there to remind my relatives of the livestock they once had. I peer closer, and on each there is a small label - goat, horse, cow.

Numbly shaking my head, I walk back to the house. We speak in hushed tones, discussing the war and the friends we have lost.

As dusk falls, a single candle is lit. The world outside is almost silent, and I have an eerie feeling that we are drifting alone, surrounded by sussurating space.

Shears

I make a daring escape from a maximum security prison camp, and, after effecting my egress from the moist tunnel, plunge headlong into the trunky darkness of the serried conifers that encircle these regions.

I scramble beneath the needled branches for some time before I realise I have a pair of garden shears embedded in my stomach, the weathered handles protruding in the direction of my escape. I attempt to wrench them from my flesh, but the pain is too great. Reluctantly I leave the shears in my belly, and stumble onwards.

With deepening anxiety, I become slowly aware that with each step, the blades of the shears move infinitesimally closer, cutting into something vital that is deep inside me.

I have no choice but to continue, and as dusk cloaks the forests I finally emerge into the open plains. I climb, with panting breaths, a ridge and stand there, horribly conscious, gazing towards a dubious future. The shears are almost closed.

A Bit Worried Today

Murder

Someone standing close to me is shot in the neck. He spins round suddenly very slowly and I can see the hole in his neck where his Adam's apple should be. It is edited like a scene from a film. The crowd scatters and meshes and the man falls. Bad thoughts crowd my head. But the worst thing is that I want to get away as quickly as I can and I can't remember where I have left my coat.

Sweaters

We listen to the radio sometimes and the politicians and the generals all seem to be okay. They can't commit and often they can't comment either but we often have to do both.

When this is over we will watch the news. Then the politicians will be more precise. They will have novel ways of arranging events. Everything will be okay, and that will be official. It would be hard, otherwise, to tell what had happened.

Warehouses

The children play along the canal where the warehouses used to be. They have elaborate games and run across planks over the water. They don't mind when the helicopters come over because they have got used to them.

Look, I say. That's where Homebase used to be. They are not interested. It's not their fault. Maybe it's mine.

Perspective

Life in our city becomes intolerable and we have to get out. It is very difficult.

We escape to the countryside on the slopes outside the town. But none of the people who live in the country want to help us. We are bringing the plague. I look down at our city. Everything looks strange and perspective doesn't work any more.

We climb the hills into the woods and we really don't know what is going to happen to us.

Exclamation

Some of the days that go by should have exclamation marks after them. Yesterday had photorealistic houses but painted flames coming from the roofs. I saw it from up on the hill!

Explosions

Almost everybody I know is insane. They have been concealing it with varying degrees of success for a long time. They are calm during explosions and I can tell that they don't want to be. I heard the craziest thing about someone I know but I can't write it down because that would be bad. So here I am, in the woods.

Popping

Nothing like this could ever happen to me that is happening to me. I'm in a dream this isn't really happening.

To my right [closeup] [in detail] a muddied foot in a brutal boot [once a soft baby foot kissed and dried] [who are you why are you] mud on my cuff in my palm. Staring at my wrist under the boot. My writing wrist my drawing wrist with just a little arthritis how can I ever have worried about that. Back of my wrist feeling gravel under the mud worse and worse [booted muddied bloodied foot rocking twisting] [rockabye what is your name] water in my eyes like needles.

And [too loud] [in detail] a cracking and popping.

Not Worried

When things like this are going on it seems luxurious to consider my own responses to them. In the valley the flames are smudges of yellow but I still perambulate around my feelings of horror and disbelief. I used to live there but now I don't. Now I don't live anywhere.

Are you worried? Because I'm not.

Except

A lot of the houses out here are bright red, straight out of the paint tube. The fences around their gardens aren't right. But over there, to the east, everything is realistic and local and as it should be, except on fire.

Partly Mechanical Hardly Human

Stupid Hill

Even though everyone has been here before, even though there's a souvenir shop, even though the tracks are concreted, and even though there is taped commentary. To your left you will see, to your right is, and if you use a little imagination you could, thank you, please move along to the next commentary point.

In my dream this hill was lonely and grassgreen, there were maybe three trees on the top, with me on my own, and I can't remember climbing up.

In real life there is a coach park and easy access from the motorway, in real life there is an experience to experience, in real life there is a McDonalds and a carpark and a sign saying coming soon TGI Fridays. In real life there are ascents graded according to difficulty, there is a big chairlift thing if the effort is too much.

Would you please move along to the next commentary point, refreshments are available, there is a cafeteria, there is a gift store, there are authentic re-enactments of authentic events in history.

What am I doing on this stupid hill?

Dead Now

And after all the parties and the reunions and those funerals and everything, I remembered that we had buried a time capsule. Perhaps we were already old friends when we had the plan; fill a sealed box with our secrets and bury it. I think the idea was to dig it up when all our secrets had become aged and meaningless and didn't hurt and couldn't break anything.

I'm here now typing on my computer.

Same old, same old.

My language isn't necessary at all.

Everything has to go out.

I feel like a dunce.

I've landed on an alien world.

Life is a seedy, dirty, nasty thing, but it has to be covered. My life is pretty much covered with accidents, disasters, mistakes; all small, all inconsequential. Nothing I've done would interest you. I buried my secrets.

My life was, you know, great and interesting and everything. And awful and unbelievable and terrible.

And exciting. And boring. Over.

Shit Painting

This was when I still wanted to be a painter; just before I concluded that I was destined to take any job that came my way.

Ha ha! Pick the paints with the best names. *Cerulean Disregard. Jerusalem Pointless. Scarlet Disaster. Burnt House. Titanium Weapon. Hurt Child.* What else? Oh, some easy targets, some cigarettes, toys, cities, fur.

Rows of dead people in sportswear.

Nike Nike Nike.

Jerrybuilt export processing zones on fire.

And it was supposed to be a diary of a bad painting. Which might even be mildly amusing, if I'd actually got round to painting anything. Ha ha!

Beautiful Story About

There's just the muffled crunchy sound of teeth grinding and scraping of boots on tarmac, or something, and a noise far away that maybe is someone crying or a cat. And everything moves a bit in the wind, but there isn't any noise.

There's a tape on of people talking about probably nothing important at a restaurant, and a marching sound that's a bit like a lot of soldiers and a bit like a wheel rubbing against metal. But it might not be a tape - it's hard to tell. And everyone's run out of jokes because no-one's laughing at anything, although they probably would if they had a sense of humour.

Probably nothing important. Just a noise in the dark when you're half-asleep, something behind the curtains. Don't look it's nothing. Don't look. Honestly, it's nothing.

Maybe it's the town you live in making these noises, or maybe it's you. Just a million mobiles and modems, squawking and spluttering and hissing like piss on a fire. Like a million gallons of piss on an inferno. Just think of that, eh? Just think of that.

Vertebrae being sawn apart sounds like this.

And when I opened the curtains they were taking the set away and packing up for the day; the cameras and lights turned off. The darkness replaced with striplights and grey skies, the blind whirring of machinery.

I'd like to write a beautiful story about love:

Only A Nightmare

What's the idea? This is the idea: you get into your car that you bought this year on some huge mortgage scheme and will have to replace in another year or so after you've killed a few birds mammals and maybe a child or two and drive to the supermarket past all the dead shops that have been put out of business by the supermarket and park on a huge expanse of concrete that has been put on a field or a wood then walk probably further than you would to a corner shop and commandeer a huge trolley and go into the supermarket and fill up the trolley with things you don't want don't need and can't afford then have an argument with whoever you're with because the whole experience is beginning to destroy you and then you queue up behind a line of similarly soul-damaged people then a poor unfortunate kid or pensioner who probably dreams in bleeps reads the barcodes on everything and doesn't want to hear you say anything and is obliged to ask you if you have a loyalty card and if you want cashback *(yes please I'll have the fucking lot back and you can keep all this crap in my trolley)* then you have to cart it all back to your car and load it up in the boot and get in and get out of the gargantuan carpark then drive home through the bleak wasteland occupied only by those too poor to own a car and unload it all again into your dream home and then consume it all and when you've shat it all out you have to fucking go back again.

Rural Idyll

She said that the couple who own the shop are nosey and given to gossip. If I went to the shop there would be talk in the village, she said. There had been a power cut and I thought it would be a good idea to get some candles in case it happened again.

The shop was shut and it was cold so I didn't hang around. I walked around in the empty village and there wasn't much to see. Some of the houses showed evidence of having once been shops also; there was a plinth and a cross that seemed to suggest a former market place. Sometimes a car went past. But mostly there was just me and my thoughts and a grey sky overhead that may have indicated rain. The rain didn't come which was sort of good and sort of bad.

By the time I got back to the shop it had opened, so I went in and I was the only person in it except for the couple who owned it. And they just looked at me silently in the kind of way you can feel even when your back is turned.

I got the candles and it was maybe quite exciting to hear the talk in the village after I'd gone but I doubt it.

Designer Outlet Village

I am too late, I am too old, I am late. Perhaps I am apprehensive and weary. We drink coffee from paper cups while we sit in a polystyrene mediæval castle. There aren't many people.

The Burger King has a thatched roof and I briefly wonder about the employment prospects for thatchers in this wet, cold and foggy part of the country. I once wanted to be a thatcher, but today I am glad I am a nothing. Whatever. There is a glass roof arching over everything here anyway. And I wouldn't want to thatch a Burger King in a polystyrene castle.

Motorway on such a grey day with fog, and the town we drove through was dead, and then a sliproad and huge signs loom out of the fog saying designer outlet village. We park in the carpark with the other cars.

After walking to the designer outlet village there is music outside in the fog, but it isn't very good music and even without fog it wouldn't be very good. Inside there are a lot of clothes to buy but I don't buy any because they aren't very good. There are a few people from the dead town here and they aren't buying any of the clothes either.

Everyone is very subdued.

This is quite nice, she says to me, holding something with sleeves up for me to look at, but I can't find any words. Perhaps I am apprehensive and weary.

We drink coffee from paper cups while we sit in a polystyrene mediæval castle.

For Modern Living

Always sunny where we live, in old thatched cottages, extensively refurbished, by the pond. Ducks quacking, birds singing, a shiny lowslung German car crunching on the gravel.

Sunlight always on our backs, always blue skies, never rain. A bounding labrador on Sunday walks, no mental illness.

Always sunny, glowing round our hair like haloes. Stress is so yesterday, disappointment so passé. Always he = *charm* + *smiles,* she = *tilts head to him*: they laugh. Always active in leisure pursuits and work.

We always cook the latest fashions, we always wear sturdy-but-stylish. Our taste is impeccable, our skins flawless *[he = slightly rugged: her = english rose w/attitude]*.

Always sunny where we live, in loft conversions, architect designed, in an up-and-coming area, mobiles cheeping, emails incoming.

My wife?
Works in outsourcing you must meet her.

My suit? Thank you.

Really? I was talking to them only last week, haven't you heard?

Cappuccinos, meetings.

115

Here's my car, my wide car, with the marque, the shine, the model that tells you my approximate income bracket.

Always sunny.

I am effective - *brutally effective* - in meetings.

Money makes money, money meets money, money greets money, in atriums, lifts and restaurants.

I get shown the wine label.

I know what I'm talking about.

I finish with a coffee and a smile.

Always take the money always run.

Always sunny where we live.

No silences in our conversations

[modern life where everything is possible].

Two Substances

Snuff

We loved each other so much that sometimes it hurt, even when we were close. I wanted to be her and she wanted to be me. Sex never felt complete, and afterwards we talked carelessly about easy subjects to avoid discussing the ache that bruised us both. So one day, in the kitchen, she cut me and I cut her; gently, slowly, too easily. It was the knife we used for onions and our tears were painful but expectant. We dripped the blood into coffee mugs, then bandaged up and went to bed. We fucked and there were stars but we saw different constellations.

The next day the blood was dry and rusty in the mugs. We scraped it diligently onto sheets of paper. We looked at each other silently and lowered our heads to snort each other's dust. Afterwards we both carried a pouch of powdered blood, and when we were low and apart we would retire to a restroom and sniff, sniff, sniff.

Oh my darling, we went on and on. Our blood was there always, red and viscous, burnt ochre and blowaway. My blood in your nasal membranes, filtering into your capillaries, finding its inexorable way to your heart. Your blood. My nose. My heart. We belonged to each other and we had made our love tangible, real; something that could be weighed and consumed, taken and enjoyed.

It wasn't a surprise when we used the scalpel to shave flesh from each other's upper arms. We dried the flesh, though it was difficult to dessicate it completely. We used the airing cupboard. The powdered flesh was better; cocaine to blood's speed.

Did it end badly? Did we go too far? Was our love replaced or deleted by want or need? In losing ourselves in each other did we lose the essence in ourselves that the other loved? Did time simply bore us with its slow wearing-down?

I have no answers to any of those questions. But now, sitting here in the kitchen, I admit I am scared of the knife, that I can't dig deeply enough to draw blood, that I will have nothing in the morning but red, raised scratches on my arm. I don't want her to cut me.

Did we kill each other, or are we living happily; but only as happily as you are?

Condiment

So one day I began collecting: I urinated into a large jar. I masturbated and scooped my ejaculate into a second jar. I took a knife from the drawer and made an incision on the end of my finger and squeezed the blood in thin trickles and fat drops into a third jar. I sat down with a fourth jar on my lap, and thought of sad things. Then I wept into the jar.

I repeated these actions every evening, each fluid into its appointed jar. After a month, I emptied the contents of the jars into small saucepans, which I heated carefully until I had evaporated the liquid. When the pans had cooled, I scraped the residue, with the aid of a funnel, into separate salt cellars. I then tasted each of my personal salts, judging which would go best with what food.

My experiment was a resounding success. The salts seemed to impart a subtle intensity to spicy dishes, and a freshness and zest to even the most homely soup. And so my restaurant began to attract many more patrons as increasing numbers of adulatory reviews appeared in some of the Sunday supplements.

Obviously, I had to continue to produce the salts that had made my culinary creations such overnight successes. My establishment was now being patronised by celebrities as well as politicians and the merely rich.

My difficulty lay chiefly with eliciting sadness on demand. On some nights I would sit in my chair, the fourth jar on my lap, and start laughing with joy at the success of my restaurant. I would have to force myself to envisage a starving child or departing lover. I knew that there was boundless, ceaseless suffering on this Earth, but I found it more and more difficult to identify with it myself, while the prestige of my restaurant grew higher, and with it my bank balance.

I found that the most efficacious manner of forcing tears from my eyes was to think of love; loves lost, love's tragedies, and love's hopelessness. And so it was that I began to have trouble with the second jar. Latterly, my attempts at masturbation were rather more difficult, as my erotic thoughts staggered and tumbled into the despair I needed for the fourth jar. Not infrequently, I found it impossible to distinguish between sorrow and love.

After five months, I caught myself ejaculating into my lap, upon which rested the jar meant for tears. I began to find sorrow arousing, and could not cry without getting an erection. Conversely, I could not find a woman attractive without starting to weep.

I worried about my salts, for my supplies were running low. Moreover, the quality of the salt from the first jar was beginning to decline, as I attempted to find solace in alcoholic abandon. I would drink deeply; and laugh, and cry. But my urine suffered. It became thin and pale, copious but worthless. The salt I extracted was tasteless.

The reputation of my restaurant would keep its fortunes buoyant for a while, but I knew that sooner, rather than later, the decline in the quality of the seasonings would be noted. I sank lower into despair. I could not run the terrible risk of sharing my secret with anyone else. I had only one reliable source of salt - that which filled the third jar. The third jar never ran out. The menu had to reflect this, and there was a preponderance of rich, red, meaty dishes, lavishly enhanced with the salt of my blood, trickled - or sometimes drunkenly spurted, gushed - from my fingers, thumbs, wrists or arms every evening. But I was weakening.

My drinking was becoming uncontrollable, I would involuntarily orgasm during the news, and burst into tears at the most inopportune moments. The constant bloodletting was making me anaemic.

I resolved to return to the formula that had won my eaterie so many plaudits. Determinedly, I researched the most emotionally draining novels, the most haunting poems. I ejaculated again and again into the second jar. I drank pure fruit juice and mineral water and produced once again the golden, viscous urine that filled the first jar. I wept uncontrollably, for three-quarters of a hour, with a pornographic magazine propped in front of me. And I took the sharpest knife and drew one widening red line across my wrist.

The banquet was a success.